What Will the Weather Be Like Today?

Also illustrated by Kazuko
Cuckoobush Farm

Also by Paul Rogers
From Me to You

What Will the Weather Be Like Today?

PAUL ROGERS
PICTURES BY KAZUKO

Macmillan/McGraw-Hill School Publishing Company
New York Chicago Columbus

Pour la famille Bony
P.R.

To my mother
From Kazuko

Macmillan/McGraw-Hill School Division
10 Union Square East
New York, New York 10003

Printed and bound in Mexico.
ISBN 0-02-274903-9

12 13 14 15 16 17 18 19 20 REY 99 98 97

Just at the moment
when night becomes day,
when the stars in the sky
begin fading away,

you can hear all the birds
and the animals say,

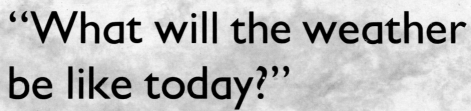

"What will the weather be like today?"

Will it be windy?

Will it be warm?

Will there be snow?

Or a frost?

Or a storm?

"Be dry," says the lizard, "and I won't complain."

The frog in the bog says,
"Perhaps it will rain."

The white cockatoo
likes it steamy and hot.

The mole doesn't know
if it's raining or not.

"Whatever the weather,
I work," says the bee.

"Wet," says the duck,
"is the weather for me."

"Weather? What's that?"

say the fish in the sea.

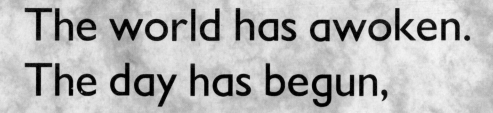

The world has awoken.
The day has begun,

and somewhere it's cloudy,

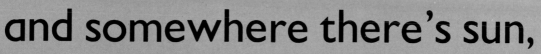
and somewhere there's sun,

and somewhere the sun
and the rain meet to play,

and paint a bright rainbow
to dress up the day!

How is the weather where *you* are today?